D0426594

JUL - - 2011

Veronika Martenova Charles

Illustrated by David Parkins

TUNDRA BOOKS

Text copyright © 2010 by Veronika Martenova Charles
Illustrations copyright © 2010 by David Parkins

Published in Canada by Tundra Books,
75 Sherbourne Street, Toronto, Ontario M5A 2P9

Published in the United States by Tundra Books of Northern New York,
P.O. Box 1030, Plattsburgh, New York 12901

Library of Congress Control Number: 2009938443

All rights reserved. The use of any part of this publication reproduced, transmitted in any form or by any means, electronic, mechanical, photocopying, recording, or otherwise, or stored in a retrieval system, without the prior written consent of the publisher – or, in case of photocopying or other reprographic copying, a licence from the Canadian Copyright Licensing Agency – is an infringement of the copyright law.

Library and Archives Canada Cataloguing in Publication

Charles, Veronika Martenova
It's not about the rose! / Veronika Martenova
Charles ; illustrated by David Parkins.

(Easy-to-read wonder tales)
ISBN 978-0-88776-954-2

1. Fairy tales. 2. Children's stories, Canadian (English).
I. Parkins, David II. Title. III. Series: Charles, Veronika
Martenova. Easy-to-read wonder tales.

PS8555.H42242I8775 2010 jC813'.54 C2009-905862-6

We acknowledge the financial support of the Government of Canada through the Book Publishing Industry Development Program (BPIDP) and that of the Government of Ontario through the Ontario Media Development Corporation's Ontario Book Initiative. We further acknowledge the support of the Canada Council for the Arts and the Ontario Arts Council for our publishing program.

Printed and bound in Canada

1 2 3 4 5 6 15 14 13 12 11 10

CONTENTS

YARD SALE
PART 1

"We are having a yard sale today,"

Ben told Lily and Jake.

"I wonder if people

will buy anything."

"What's this flower under glass?"

asked Lily.

"That's the magic rose from

Beauty and the Beast," said Ben.

"The rose wasn't magic," Jake said.

"Yes, it was," said Ben.

"It kept dropping petals until the

prince was twenty-one years old."

"That's not how it goes,"

said Jake.

"A girl asks her father for a rose...

Wait. I'll tell you the story."

BELLA AND THE BEAST

(*Beauty and the Beast* from Europe)

Once there was a man

who had three daughters.

One day he had to go

on a journey.

“What shall I bring you back?”

he asked his daughters.

“I would like a golden dress,”

said the oldest daughter.

“I would like a silver necklace,”

said the second one.

"Bring yourself back, Father,"

said Bella, the youngest daughter.

"That's what I want the most."

"But, child," said her father,

"you must ask for something."

"Then, I'd like a rose," she said.

The father brought the presents,

but he couldn't find a rose.

On his way home

he passed by a garden.

Maybe I'll find a rose there,

the father thought.

He spied a rose bush

and plucked one pretty flower.

All at once he heard thunder,

and an ugly beast appeared.

"How dare you steal my roses!"

said the beast.

"Forgive me, but my daughter

asked for one. It's only

a single rose," said the man.

"Stealing is stealing, whether it's

a jewel or a flower. You'll pay

with your life," said the beast.

"Please, sir, let me go,"

pleaded the father.

"There's no one else

to take care of my daughters."

"Well," said the beast,

"I will spare your life,

but you must bring me the girl

who asked for the rose."

"I promise," said the father.

At home, the man gave

his daughters their presents.

"Why are you so sad?"

Bella asked.

So, her father told her about

the beast and his promise.

"It's all my fault," said Bella,

"and a promise is a promise.

I must go with you to the beast."

The next day, Bella and her father

went to the beast's mansion.

"Are you willing to stay here?"

the beast asked Bella.

Bella was frightened,

but she answered, "Yes."

"Then, this is your home now,"

said the beast.

Bella stayed at the mansion,

but soon she became lonely.

When the beast came by,

she began to talk with him.

Bella thought the beast was kind,

and she grew to like his company.

One morning the beast said,

“You may visit your father.

But come back tomorrow,

or I will die without you.”

Bella went home.

She was so glad to see her father,

that the time just flew by.

She stayed too long.

When Bella returned to the mansion

the beast was not there.

"Where are you?" she called,

but there was no reply.

She went into the garden.

Under the rose bush lay the beast.

He was dying.

Bella fell down beside him, crying.

"Oh beast, please don't die.

I love you."

As soon as she said it,

the beast's skin split open

and a young man appeared.

“Where is the beast?” she asked.

“It’s me,” the young man told her.

“You freed me from an evil spell!”

They sent for Bella’s family,

and they all lived happily together.

Lily reached out and picked up

the rose under glass.

"This could be the rose

that Bella asked for," she said.

"Maybe she saved it because

that's how she met the beast.

My mom always saves memories."

Ben pulled out a toy

from the pile.

"Look at this lizard," he said.

"It reminds me of another story

of a girl who marries a monster.

But it was a lizard. Listen ...."

THE LIZARD

(*Beauty and the Beast* from Indonesia)

Once there was an old woman
who lived in the jungle.
She had raised a lizard as if
he was her own child.
When the lizard grew up, he said,
"Mother, please go
to our neighbors' house
where the seven sisters live.
Ask the oldest one
if she will be my wife."

The old woman took a gift
for the girl and off she went.
When she arrived,
she climbed the ladder
and sat down.

"Why have you come?"

asked the eldest girl.

"Well," said the old woman,

"I have come to offer you a gift

and ask you to marry my lizard."

"Marry a lizard?" the girl replied.

"What would I do with a lizard?"

The girl pushed the old woman
out the door so hard
that she fell down the ladder.
The old woman picked herself up
and went home.

"Did she say yes?"

asked the lizard.

"No," said the old woman.

"The girl has no use for a lizard."

"Don't mind her," said the lizard.

"Go back there again

and ask the other sisters."

Five more times the woman returned,

and each time she was refused.

But the youngest sister, Lia,

felt sorry for her, so she agreed.

The following day, the old woman

took the lizard to Lia's house.

Lia put a mat on the floor

and spread out her wedding gifts.

She gave the old woman a feast.

When the woman left, the lizard

remained as Lia's husband.

The older sisters were disgusted.
They wiped the mud from their feet
on the lizard's back and teased,
"Lia can't help us make a garden.
She must take care of her lizard."
"Hush!" Lia told them,
and she washed the lizard clean.

When the sisters went out to make

a clearing for their garden,

the lizard said to Lia,

"Let's make our own garden."

Lia put the lizard in a basket

and went into the jungle.

"Put me down," said the lizard.

He ran around the mountain,
lashing the grass with his tail.
With one blow, he cut down trees.
Then he prepared the ground
for planting. When Lia's sisters
saw this, they were amazed.

At home, the sisters told Lia,

"Don't come to the planting feast.

Your husband is an ugly lizard."

Then, they wiped mud on him again.

"Don't be sad," the lizard told Lia,

"We *will* go to the feast. Take me

to the river and we'll get ready."

At the river the lizard said,

“Now, throw me into the water!”

“Why?” asked Lia. “I like you.

I want you to stay with me.”

But the lizard insisted,

so she did as he asked.

The lizard plunged into the water

and when he emerged,

he had changed into a man.

Lia was amazed.

In the evening, all dressed up,

Lia and her lizard-husband

went to the festival.

"Who are they?" asked the sisters

when they saw the couple coming.

“That’s Lia with her husband,”

the old woman replied.

“We always knew he was special!”

the sisters cried. They ran

to meet him, but he would have

nothing to do with them.

Later, Lia's husband built a house

high on the mountain

and lived there with Lia and

his mother ever after.

★ ★ ★

"I know a story about a girl

who married a bear!" said Lily.

"The bear was under a spell

just like Bella's prince

in *Beauty and the Beast*.

But in the story I know,

the bear had to leave,

and the girl had look for him.

I'll tell it to you."

THE WHITE BEAR

(*Beauty and the Beast* from

Norway)

There was once a man and a woman

who had many children,

but they didn't have much food

or clothing to give them.

The children were all pretty,

but the youngest daughter, Thora,

was the prettiest.

One evening, the weather was wild.

It was raining hard,

and the wind shook the cottage

as the family sat inside.

All at once, they heard three taps

on the window.

The father went out

and saw a big, white bear.

“Good evening,” said the bear.

“The same to you,” said the man.

“May I marry your youngest girl?

If she comes with me, I will

make you rich,” said the bear.

"Come back in a week,"
the father told the white bear.
Then he asked his daughter,
"Could you live with the bear
to help your family?"
When the bear came back,
Thora decided to go with him.

She climbed upon his back
and off they went.
They rode a long, long way
until they came to a castle.

There were many rooms, and

warm food was waiting for them.

After Thora had eaten,

she went to bed.

At night, the white bear came

and lay down beside her.

But he had changed into a man.

Thora couldn’t see his face,

because he left before sunrise.

Each night was the same.

After a few months,

Thora began to miss her family.

She told the bear about it.

"I'll take you to visit them,

but promise not to talk about me.

It would bring bad luck to us."

The next day, Thora and the bear traveled a long, long way, until they came to a grand house. “Your family lives here, now,” said the bear. Then he left.

Thora was happy,

and she told her family

that she had everything

she had ever wished for.

But her mother wanted

to talk alone with her.

"Now tell me about the bear,"
she said. "It's just between us."
So Thora told her how the bear
changed into a man at night
and how she wished she knew
what he looked like.

"It may be a troll you're with,"

the mother worried.

She gave Thora a candle saying,

"Light it when he's asleep."

Soon the bear came for Thora

and took her back to the castle.

That night while the bear slept,

Thora lit the candle to see him.

He was so handsome

that Thora bent to kiss him.

As she did, hot wax

dripped on him and he woke up.

"What have you done?" he cried.

"If only you had kept our secret

for another year, the evil spell

would have been broken.

A troll princess punished me

because I didn't want her.

Now I will have to marry her."

"What can I do now?" asked Thora.

"Try to find me ...." he said.

All at once, a thick fog wrapped around them. When it cleared up, the bear and the castle were gone, and Thora lay in the woods.

She set out and walked for days,

until she came to a cave.

Inside, sat an old woman,

playing with a golden apple.

"Have you seen a white bear?"

asked Thora. "I need to find him."

"Yes, he came by,"

the woman replied.

"Perhaps I can help you.

I'll lend you my horse

and give you this golden apple.

The horse knows the way."

Thora thanked her.

She rode a long, long time,

until she came to a castle

at the end of the earth.

Thora rested near a castle window

and began to play

with the golden apple.

The troll princess looked out.

"How much for the apple?"

she asked.

"It's not for sale," Thora answered.

"Then, what do you want for it?"

asked the troll.

“I want to sleep outside

the bear’s bedroom,” said Thora.

“Fine,” said the troll princess.

“Come back this evening.”

That night, Thora lay down

outside the white bear’s door.

When everyone in the castle
was asleep, she began to speak.
The white bear heard her,
and he opened the door.

"You came just in time," he said.

"I almost had to marry the troll.

Now that you've found me,

I'm free from the spell."

Then, they mounted the horse,

and set off back home.

YARD SALE PART 2

“How much is this rose?”

Lily asked Ben.

“I’ll find out,” said Ben.

His mother came over.

“Ben says you like the rose.

You may have it if you want,”

she said.

“Hey, Ben,” said Jake.

“How much do you want

for the lizard?”

"It will be a dollar," said Ben.

"How about fifty cents?

I'll bring it to you tomorrow,"

Jake said.

"Okay," said Ben. "But remember,

a promise is a promise!"

ABOUT THE STORIES

Beauty and the Beast stories are found all over the world. People know the Disney version best, but it is not the only one.

Bella and the Beast represents European versions of the theme. My telling is based on Joseph Jacobs' *Beauty and the Beast,* which is a blend of several European sources.

The Lizard is a retelling of an Indonesian story, *The Lizard Husband.*

White Bear is based on a Norwegian folktale called *East of the Sun and West of the Moon.*